WELCOME TO THE WORLD OF PARANORMAL INVESTIGATIONS

Copyright© 2020. David Flowers

All rights reserved. No part of this work covered by the copyright herein may be reproduced or used in any form or by any means—graphic, electronic or mechanical without the prior written permission of the publisher. Any request for photocopying, recording, taping, or information storage and retrieval systems of any part of this book shall be directed in writing to Ms. Ping Du.

Extreme care has been taken to trace the ownership of copyright material contained in this book. The publisher will gladly receive any information that will enable them to rectify any reference or credit line in subsequent editions.

This publication contains the opinions and ideas of its author and is designed to provide useful advice in regard to the subject matter covered.

DEDICATION

This book is dedicated to my little sister Ryda Widener without whom I couldn't have done this.

I would also like to thank my wife, Emily Flowers, and kids, Eddie Joe Matish, Elly Matish, and James Flowers. Thank you for putting up with my shenanigans and dad jokes throughout the years and being supportive, even when you thought I was crazy. And to the many paranormal investigators I've met over my many years in the paranormal field. Many of whom I have learned a great deal from.

ACKNOWLEDGMENTS

I can't go any further without acknowledging the following people whom I've had the privilege to investigate with, and our experiences helped me write this book. I am proud to call these people my friends.

John Stephens – Paranormal Investigator and Co-Founder of Virginia Paranormal Events. You have done more to spread the word about paranormal activity and locations, in Virginia and the surrounding states, than anyone I know personally.

Michelle Bennett and Vicki Wunderale – Two of the OG's with Virginia Paranormal Occurrence Research – Thank you for the years of friendship and our many investigations together.

Cherie Bryant – You are a fun lady to investigate with.

Geri Pritchard Reyes – Psychic / Medium – You are a wild and crazy lady and my go-to for the metaphysical parts of the paranormal world.

Phil and JahNette Payette – Tidewater & Albemarle Paranormal – Phil, a U.S. Navy Veteran, I really appreciate your analytical approach to an investigation. Thank you for your service to our country. JahNette, Psychic / Medium. You opened my eyes to the psychic world. You almost made me wreck while I was driving when you did it, but you opened them up. Thank you.

Jason Britt and Jonathan Elliott Foley – U.S. Marine Veterans who I've had the pleasure of investigating with a few times. Thank you for your service to our country.

INTRODUCTION

I'm David; I am the founder and lead investigator for Virginia Paranormal Occurrence Research. I did my very first "Ghost Hunt" over 30 years ago when I was in high school, and I got the mess scared out of me because I didn't know what I was doing. I just went out to an old, abandoned farmhouse looking for ghosts. When I saw a chair rocking with no one in it, it scared me, but I was hooked.

Over the years, I have met numerous Paranormal Investigators and even more Ghost Hunters. There is a difference between the two. An investigator is looking for who, what, when, where, and how of what is happening. A ghost hunter is just looking for the experience. There is nothing wrong with being a ghost hunter; you just don't get answers.

For everyone I've met in person, I've probably made contact, online, with three or four more. Some of them have the same mindset as I do, and some not so much but to each their own. Not to say they are wrong, and my way is the only way because that couldn't be farther from the truth. Just because I may not agree with someone about the way they approach an investigation doesn't mean they are wrong. Differences aside, I try to learn from everyone I meet.

There is a lot more to a paranormal investigation than just putting on a fancy black t-shirt, picking up your camera, a digital voice recorder, a K-II meter, a ghost box, and go rushing into a creepy old building expecting to talk to someone who died there or something. That is ghost hunting, not a paranormal investigation. That is a lot of fun, but you do not get any answers doing that. You need to do your homework. Ask questions. You need to research the location, the residence past, and the present, especially if you are part of a group that provides private investigations in people's homes. Most of the clients who contact your group want you to find answers for them. Is it grandma just sticking around keeping an eye on things, or is it something more sinister? Even if you are not with a group that provides this service, it's still a good idea to know what you may be getting yourself into.

The purpose of this book is to help guide the novice down the correct path into safe and ethical investigations and to maybe remind some of the more experienced investigators of something they may have forgotten over the years. Even though I have been doing this for several years, I still consider myself a student of the paranormal. I have spent countless hours researching the different aspects of paranormal investigation. In this book, I'm going to use my years of experience to go over the who, what, when, where, and how-to of paranormal investigations. I always like to talk with others to maybe learn a new technique or a new source for research. I am a complete supporter of paranormal unity. If other investigators or groups come up to me wanting to exchange ideas or looking for info, I jump at the opportunity. The more you network, the more you can learn.

In the pages that follow, I will be talking a little bit about private residence investigations. The bottom line is, just because you read this, it does not automatically make you qualified to lead a private residential investigation. The only thing that will qualify you to lead private investigations is OJT (On the Job Training). Cut your teeth on public investigations. Get with an established team, learn how they handle things. Make contacts with people who are able to help you out with situations you may not be completely comfortable with. You may want to stick with public investigations only, and that is perfectly fine. There are many people out there in the same boat.

I sincerely hope you get some enjoyment and learn something from the pages that follow. Now, let's get started.

CONTENTS

DEDICATION..i

ACKNOWLEDGMENTS...iii

INTRODUCTION..iv

THE BASICS..1

EQUIPMENT..7

METAPHYSICAL...22

TYPES OF HAUNTINGS...27

TYPES OF OCCURRENCES..31

RESEARCH..38

THE INVESTIGATION..40

REVIEW AND REVEAL..57

AUTHOR'S NOTE..59

PARANORMAL GLOSSARY / DICTIONARY................60

THE BASICS

1. Be Professional – If you are investigating at a private residence or public location, you want to look as professional as you can. You are not only representing yourself and your team, but in essence, you are also representing the entire paranormal field.

Dress appropriately. You don't have to dress in your Sunday best, but you shouldn't wear a shirt with inappropriate images or wording either. Also, there is no need to go around swearing like a drunken sailor either. Sure, some things may happen to startle you or something, and an occasional cuss word will slip out. I'm not really talking about that. It happens to a lot of us. I'm talking about going around saying "F" this and "F" that, especially if you are doing a private residence or on a public ghost hunt with other people around.

When you go to the investigation, it's ok to take your entire arsenal with you. You never know what you are going to need other than cameras and voice recorders until the time of the investigation. However, one thing you do not want to do is unpack everything you have before the investigation. You know what you have, and you should know where it's at. By unpacking everything, it takes up an unnecessary room, and it makes your base of operations look cluttered and messy. To some, it may look as if you are trying to show off. If you are using a corded DVR system, you should coil up any excess cords and cables. It makes things look neater as well as makes things safer if you have cords and cables on the floor.

2. Be Skeptical – It is extremely important to try to disprove or "debunk" every single thing you see and hear. Probably about 90 to 95 percent of everything you come across will have some sort of non-paranormal explanation. Remember, you will be spending the majority of your time in the dark. When in the dark, your senses start to rise. You will hear a lot more than you do during the daytime when there is a lot of human contamination. You will hear things like the wind blowing through a window or a door that has been left partially open, or the building you are in may start to settle. Even if it is an old building, they still settle due to temperature and humidity changes. Once your eyes get used to the dark, you will see a lot more, too but remember, even though it is nighttime, you can still encounter shadows even from the slightest of light. So always be aware of your surroundings.

3. Dress Appropriately – Always remember to dress appropriately, and not only for the being professional aspect of it. Dress comfortably in accordance with your surroundings. If you are in a field such as an old battlefield or something where the grass and weeds can get a bit high, you may want to wear long pants in case there are thorny plants you may walk through. Depending on the time of year, if you start during the day and the temp is warm, and you continue into the night, and the temp cools off, have a jacket or hoodie standing by. If you are inside, make sure you are wearing sneakers or some other soft-soled shoes, so you make as little noise as possible when walking. There is nothing more frustrating than going through hours of audio files and coming across footsteps only to figure out it was one of the other investigators wearing a pair of boots or some other hard-soled shoe. Don't wear any strong-smelling colognes or perfumes. This could mask any phantom smells you may come across.

4. Safety – Safety is paramount when doing this—physical as well as spiritual. As much as we want to get irrefutable evidence of the paranormal, we need to be safe. It is not worth risking serious injury or oven death to capture that piece of evidence.

Always have a partner with you. One of you can go get help if the other is injured or needs help. If you do go out on your own, make sure someone knows where you will be. If you go to a different spot, let them know.

Say your prayers. I know some of you are not Christians, and that's fine. All religions have some sort of self-protection prayer. Whether it's the lord's prayer or whatever works for you. If you are not religious or do not prescribe to a certain religion, ground yourself. By that, I mean meditate and close yourself off to any intruder to your mental wellbeing. If you are unsure as to how to do that, you can contact a local paranormal team and ask questions. Maybe they have a team psychic or Reiki practitioner who can help you.

5. Permission – Always get permission to investigate wherever you go. Let say you are investigating an old farmhouse that has been abandoned for ten years. That farmhouse is still owned by someone, and if you are out there without permission, it is considered trespassing, and we all know that trespassing is illegal. If you don't know who owns the location you want to investigate, go to the city or county department of records. They will be able to point you in the right direction to contact the appropriate people to get permission. It is also a really good idea after you get permission to let the local police or sheriff's department know what you are doing ahead of time; that way, if they get a call in the middle of the night with a report of suspicious activity, they already know you are there, and they won't interrupt the intense EVP session you may be in the middle of.

6. Equipment – Always go through all of your equipment before every investigation to make sure it is working properly, and you have fresh batteries in everything that needs batteries. It is really frustrating when you have to stop what you are doing because of a dead battery. Make sure you have plenty of spare batteries on hand just in case of unexpected drainage.

7. Do Your Homework – Research the location. If it is an abandoned building, you can go and check out the city record of the location. If it is a building that is in use, such as an old hotel, contact the current and former employees and neighbors and see what type of occurrences they have encountered. If it's a private residence, where discretion is a must, you can get city records such as police reports from the past. The Tax Assessors Office can give you historical info on many locations you visit. Local historians are a really good source of information. They can give you the local folklore and years of what happened. This is a really important tool to help in your investigation. It helps you to determine what exactly you are looking for. It is important to note that even though you may be looking for a Civil War-era entity, you always need to keep an open mind for other things as well.

8. Drugs and Alcohol – NEVER! This is not a party. Yes, you want to enjoy what you are doing, but there is no place for drugs and alcohol in the paranormal field. They dull your senses and make it easier for bad things to happen, such as injury. If you are dealing with a negative entity, whether human or non-human, if you have been drinking or doing drugs, you cannot properly protect yourself, so just leave them alone around investigation time.

9. Know Your Surroundings – If you are doing a nighttime investigation, and most of us do, it is a really good idea to visit the location during the daylight hours so you can get a visual of the layout and also, it's a good time to get a baseline reading as far as electromagnetic fields (EMF) of location. You can look for old wiring, computers, TVs, radios, lamps, etc., anything that would give a higher EMF reading. That way, when you get there at night, you can get set up and start investigating without much delay

10. Electronics – Do your best to reduce the chance of false positives by eliminating as many electronic devices as possible. If you can, leave your cell phone at the command station or, at the very least, put it in airplane mode. If you have a camera that makes noise when you take a picture, see if you can disable that function and set it to silent. If not, at least, a voice that you are taking pictures of. That way, whoever is listening to audio will know the camera sound is not paranormal.

11. Flashlight Usage – It is important to minimize the use of your flashlight as much as possible. When you get into a space, turn your flashlight off and let your eyes adjust to the darkness. Most of the time, there should be enough ambient light so you can make your way around. When you are constantly using a flashlight, you can get false positives such as 'shadow figures.'

12. Patience – You watch all these ghost hunting TV shows, and they show a lot of things happening. You have to take into account that it is probably a 6–8 hour investigation crammed into a one-hour episode, and they may show maybe five or ten seconds of something that 'may or may not be happening.' Keep in mind that it is a TV show and who is going to tune in to a ghost hunting show when they never show anything going on. Paranormal investigating can be pretty boring. Probably the most important tool in a paranormal investigators' arsenal is your patience. You will endure all the time conducting EVP sessions and the hours sitting in silence during the investigation review, watching video footage, looking at stills, and listening to the audio files, and debunking anything that can be thrown out. It's when you do sit through all of that, and you do finally catch something, you get that excited feeling that keeps you coming back for more.

13. Stay Open-Minded – This is probably one of the most important parts. It's when you close your mind you stop learning. If someone suggests, something doesn't just automatically blow it off. It's important to remember that just because someone may have less experience than you do, it is highly possible that they may have figured something out that you never thought about. At least give it some thought and maybe even try it out once or twice to see if you get any results. No one knows everything.

14. Record Everything – Without recording everything, if something happens, as cool as it may be, all it is, is just a personal experience. A personal experience is not evidence. It is not considered evidence until you back up your experience with documentation. It's a good idea to save your recordings on some sort of external devices, such as a thumb drive or cd. I learned this the hard way.

15. Investigate Away – Keeping all the above in mind, it's time to investigate and enjoy!

16. Ethics – Last but certainly not least is your ethics. You need to remember everything you do as a 'Paranormal Investigator,' or a ghost hunter, not only reflects upon you but also reflects upon the entire paranormal field. So always make sure you are getting your permission. Never fabricate evidence. If you are at a location and you accidentally damage something, fess up to it right away, don't wait, and hope the owner doesn't find it. Again, everything you do not only puts a bad light on you but also the entire paranormal field. There are a lot of locations out there that are on the fence about allowing people to show up and conduct a ghost hunt / paranormal investigation. When someone goes around and does unethical things during the investigation, it will just make it harder for a reputable team or person to get permission later on down the road.

EQUIPMENT

Remember when you are doing a ghost hunt, and something happens, whether you hear something or if Casper himself comes up and shakes your hand if you are not recording it, you just have a personal experience. Personal experiences, however cool and exciting they may be, are not evidence.

When it comes to equipment, you can perform your investigation relatively inexpensively, or you can spend thousands of dollars. Some of the equipment works great, and some of it is just expensive toys. I am going to tell you about some of the different pieces of equipment. There are quite a few items out there that do the exact same thing, but they are called by a different name because they have one or two extra features the original didn't have. If you are anything like I am, it is not going to make any difference what I say about the equipment; you will want to test the equipment out yourself. I encourage it. Some of the things I have used in my travels I was told ahead of time that wasn't any good, but I had to find out for myself. You know what? Most of the time, they were right. But a lot of people, myself included, just need to find out firsthand. What can I say; I like gadgets!

ESSENTIALS - The following is a list of the essential items you will need to conduct your investigation:

Spare Batteries – There have been many instances where fresh batteries all of a sudden just drained for one reason or another. So, you need to make sure you have plenty of spare batteries just in case.

Cameras are a must when doing the investigation. The camera produces the best irrefutable evidence, but it can also produce some of the most controversial evidence as well. Cameras can catch things that the naked eye cannot see also catch things that you may have missed. Cameras are where you can get into your biggest expense as far as equipment is concerned. You can spend a few dollars on a small point and shoot, or you can spend a few hundred dollars on the fancier cameras with infrared (I/R) capabilities. The theory behind using I/R cameras for ghost hunting is that ghosts are more easily seen in the I/R light spectrum vs. the white light spectrum that we see-through. I am not saying you cannot see ghosts with white light because you definitely can. It's just a bit more difficult to see in the white light.

Voice Recorders are another must when doing an investigation. If you are conducting an EVP session and you think you hear something and you are not recording, then it's lost forever. With a voice recorder, you can go back and replay it as many times as necessary to determine if you did, in fact, catch something paranormal or if it was just a car driving by playing the stereo way too loud. Voice recorders also catch things that our ears cannot hear until it's played back. Again, these can be very inexpensive, or they can be well over a hundred dollars. It all depends on what kind of bells and whistles you are looking for. One very important thing to remember when you are choosing a voice recorder is to make sure it has a USB port so you can download your recordings to your computer.

EMF Meter – An EMF meter reads electromagnet fields and can be used to disprove a haunting, as well as help, substantiate experiences. Everything electrical puts off some amount of EMF, and there are a lot of people out there who are hypersensitive to EMFs. If you are in a building with older wiring that may not be up to today's codes, the wiring may be putting off higher EMFs, and if someone is hypersensitive, they may get an uneasy feeling, such as headaches, feelings of being watched all the way to nausea. It is also widely believed that ghosts also put off EMF's and an EMF meter is used to help detect that as well. There are many different types of EMF meters out there, and you just need to research them to figure out which one you like the best. Like everything else, they can be really inexpensive, or they can put you in the doghouse with your wife/husband if you spend that kind of money without telling them first. A couple of the more basic EMF meters are the K2 or the Ghost Meters.

Pen and Paper or Spare Voice Recorder is important to have just so you can make notes about what is going on around you and what you are doing when something happens. For research purposes, it's important to record the investigation conditions; that way, you can compare notes when you have an experience that has happened before.

I actually have a log that I keep when I'm conducting an investigation where I record everything from time, ambient temperature, temperature change, weather conditions, the equipment I'm using, and people I'm with, anything that may make a difference. I'd rather write it down and not need it than to not write it down and need it.

Some Sort of Time Keeping Device – We all have cell phones, but if you choose to leave your phone at the command station to reduce the chance of contamination to EMF readings, then you will need a watch to mark the time when you are starting an EVP session or when something happens such as hearing or seeing something. Remember to synchronize the time with any time and date stamps on any video equipment used.

Flashlights can be used as an investigational tool. We will get more into that later. Flashlights are important for safety purposes. The majority of the time, when you are on an investigation, you are going to be in the dark. It is best if you use a red filter on the flashlight lens. That way, there is enough light to allow you to see, but it's not so much that it messes up your night vision or any night vision cameras you are using.

First Aid Kit – It's a really good idea to always have a first aid kit on hand. Especially if you are way out somewhere and it would be really difficult to get medical help in a timely manner. Make sure it is fully stocked, before every investigation, with Band-Aids, antibiotic ointment, gauze, ace wraps, splints, etc. You never know what you may come across. You should always make sure everyone is up to speed on any medical conditions that the different people in the group may have, i.e., diabetes, epilepsy, a heart condition, etc., and make sure everyone knows what to do in a medical emergency.

OTHER ITEMS OF USE

Those were just the essentials you will need for a successful investigation. Here are a few other items you can get to help make life easier when you are on your ghost hunt and to catch the evidence we are all looking for. This is where you can really get into some money spending.

2 Way Radios – Walkie-Talkies, obviously, make it easier to contact team members. Sure, you have your cell phone, but if you are carrying them with you on your investigation, they should be in airplane mode. Plus, with Walkie Talkies, you can contact everyone at the same time instead of sending out several different texts or phone calls. Be careful when using the two ways. They will cause EMF spikes. So just be sure to make a note when they are being used.

Ghost Box – The theory behind the ghost box is that ghosts can communicate through the different radio waves in white noise. There are many different versions of the ghost box. Probably the most well-known, because they have been seen on TV for years, is the P-SB7 or P-SB11 Spirit Box by ITC Research. They scan the radio waves. The SB7 scans either AM or FM, whereas the SB11 can scan AM and FM at the same time. They both have adjustable sweep rates. Personally, I feel anything slower than 100ms gets too much radio interference. I prefer the P-SB11 myself because with that one, as I said before, you can scan AM and FM at the same time, and it also scans faster. You can scan both forward, both backward, or one forward and one backward. You can also turn off the antennae to greatly cut the chances of getting a false positive response from a local radio station. There are many skeptics out there who think that ghost boxes are a bunch of nonsense. I have used both the P-SB7 and the P-SB11, as well as some of the other lesser-known brands. You do not always catch something with them, and you have to pay really close attention when you review the data collected during an investigation to make sure you are not listening to the DJ.

Mel-Meter — The Mel-Meter is actually an EMF meter on steroids. It's digital and reads energy levels in milli-gauss or tesla. It has a red flashlight which comes in really handy. That is just one less thing you need to carry. It reads the ambient temperature, which is important if you want to compare possible paranormal occurrences to the previous occurrences. There are several different models of the Mel-Meter with different bells and whistles, such as Ambient Temperature Deviation Detector (ATDD), which is an alarm that goes off if the ambient temperature changes, up or down, by five degrees. That is important for finding cold spots. There are several more to choose from.

REM POD – The REM Pod is another version of an EMF meter, but this one has a bit of a twist to it. It actually produces an EM field, then monitors it, and when something disrupts the field, the lights and alarms go off.

BOO BUDDY – The Boo Buddy combines a REM Pod with a trigger object. In this case, its' a teddy bear, but they have come out with one that you connect via an alligator clip to a pizza pan or metal tray and put any other trigger object on it, such as a hat, a toy, or whatever.

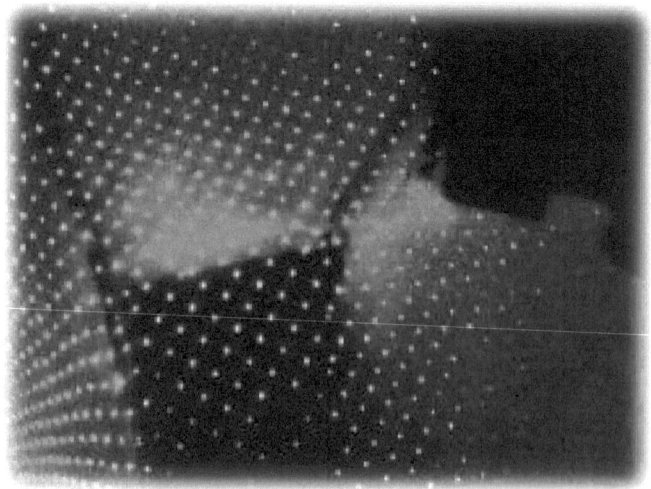

Laser Grid – The laser grid is simply a laser light with a lens on it that breaks the beam into a bunch of smaller beams. It helps to visually detect ghosts. If the ghost goes in front of it, the light beams will either dim, refract or sometimes block out. It is best to use the laser grid when you are using a video camera. Simply because during the investigation, you will not be able to see everything that is going on. It is highly possible and probable that you could catch something with the camera that you missed during the investigation/hunt.

DVR System — A DVR system is invaluable when it comes to capturing evidence. You can only be in one place at a time. With a DVR system, you can have eyes everywhere. You can get the wireless or with cables. I prefer the cables. Wireless, you have the possibility for interference which could cause a false positive. They come in 4, 8, 16, 24, and 32 channel systems. You just need to determine how many cameras you want to deal with. Remember, the more cameras you run, the video you have to sit and watch, for example, four cameras and an 8-hour investigation. That is 32 hours of video you have to watch on top of all the audio files you have to listen to. A DVR system usually comes with one 50 ft. cable per camera, so you probably will want to get an extra cable, and you can connect them together with a BNC-to-BNC coupler. The extra cables and BNC coupler are really inexpensive from AMAZON. You can get your DVR system with or without sound. If you get one without sound, it's a good idea to put a digital voice recorder with each camera; you just need to synchronize it with the time on the DVR by saying the time and channel number the recorder is located.

I/R – Full Spectrum Camcorder – It is a really good idea to have a camcorder; you are not always going to be in sight of your DVR system. With the camcorder, you can take video as well as stills. Some people prefer the Full Spectrum, saying it lets you see in all the different spectrums. Some people prefer I/R, saying that the ghosts are only visible in the I/R light spectrum and that the full spectrum causes too much clutter. But do your own research and see what best appeals to you. There are pros and cons for each.

Thermal Imaging Cameras – Thermal imaging cameras have been around for decades. I first used one back in the '80s when I was in the Navy, and I think that one was about 10 or 15 thousand dollars, and it was big and bulky. They have made many great advancements over the last few years. They are not as big and bulky as they used to be but more importantly, the prices are now way more affordable. Flir is the market leader, and they have them starting at around $150, but I definitely would not recommend that one; it's for viewing only. Then you have the TG165 for between $350 to $400. It has a 2" screen; you can take still pictures which stores them on an SD card. If you want to spend thousands of dollars, you can get the larger models that take video as well. They have fairly recently come out with units you can plug into your Android or iPhone for a couple of hundred dollars.

(Using two flashlights in tandem with a K2 Meter)

Flashlights – The flashlight is right there, close to the fence as far as being electronic or not. If you have watched any of the ghost hunting TV shows, I'm sure you have seen the flashlights being used. We are talking about just a plain Jane Maglite that you twist the head to turn on and off. You set it to where it is right between off and on, and the ghosts can use their energy to finish turning the light on or turning off. To be completely honest with you, there is a video on YouTube that describes the light and how it is not paranormal; it is no more than a coincidence. There are plenty of times I agree with this theory, except that they are only using one light. When I use the light, I am using three or four together. I will say, please turn the right one on or turn the left one on. I will also ask the same question multiple times to verify the answers. They have worked for me too many times on command for it to be a coincidence. When you are using the lights, always throw out the first couple of responses as coincidence. Then if they keep on responding after those responses, you may have something worthwhile.

Paperwork - If you are doing an investigation and not just on some fun public ghost hunt, yes, there is paperwork involved. Here is some of the paperwork you may or may not need.

Investigation Log - You may have a really good memory and can remember most of the things that happen, but there will almost always be something you may have left out. Such as what time you heard a door slam, or whatever. You will need some sort of log sheet to write down any of the different occurrences, times, temperatures, etc. That may happen during your investigation. For the majority of the paperwork, you can find some forms online at one of the many paranormal websites and download them for free use, or you can customize them to your own needs.

Investigation Report – Some groups have investigation reports as well. That way, they have easy access to the information at a certain location without having to go through all the notes, photos, and videos over and over again. Also, if you are doing a private residence, you are able to give a copy of the report to the client as well.

Permission form - Other than an investigation log, you should also have all your legal paperwork in order too. Such as proof of permission to be at a certain location. If you are at an old, abandoned farmhouse or warehouse and someone sees your flashlight, not knowing what is going on, and calls the police for some suspicious activity, it will definitely put a dampener on your night if the police show up and make you leave because you cannot show proof that you have permission to be there.

Release form - If you are planning on posting pictures or videos online, it's always a good idea to have signed release forms on file just in case someone sees their image or a picture of their property online and wants to get paid for it. The laws vary from state to state on that. It's always better to be safe than sorry.

Liability Waivers - If you are leading an investigation with other people, you need to make sure you have liability waivers signed. That way, if someone does get injured on the investigation, you won't get a surprise medical bill.

Liability Insurance – Some locations may be a little apprehensive about letting a paranormal group go traipsing around their historic property. They may be afraid you might break something or damage some of the woodwork. If you have liability insurance, that could help out a lot. It's really not that expensive either. You can get a million-dollar policy for approximately $350 per year— a small price to pay for peace of mind for both parties involved. Accidents do happen.

METAPHYSICAL

I am going to touch briefly on the metaphysical side of paranormal investigations. Many paranormal groups use psychics, mediums, or empaths during their investigations. Some people get confused and think they are all the same. But there is actually a bit of a difference.

Psychic -Being psychic, also known as being clairvoyant, means that you can perceive information that cannot be perceived through the normal senses (also called Extra Sensory Perception – ESP). This can include predicting the future, talking to non-physical beings (dead people, spirits), and being able to sense missing objects or people. Being psychic is about sensing information that other people can't usually access.

Medium - A medium is a psychic who has fine-tuned his or her Extra Sensory Perception and can communicate with the spirits in other dimensions. They are able to feel and/or hear thoughts, emotions, or mental impressions from the spirit world. A medium is able to become completely receptive to the higher frequencies or energies on which spirit people exist.

Empath - Empath means you feel other people's emotions as your own.

Suppose you are in a group that is lucky enough to have a true psychic, medium, or empath with them that is great. You do have to be very careful when it comes to this part of the paranormal. You do run into a lot of people who may have little to no metaphysical abilities, but they are making it out like they are the next Long Island Medium or something. These people can be very dangerous if you get into the wrong situation. There are plenty of people who are sensitive to this stuff. But that does not make them psychic. With the proper training, they may be able to develop the proper skill set.

PENDULUM
SAGE
DOWSING RODS

Here are some of the metaphysical tools used. These may or may not work for you. They don't work for everyone. You do not have to be a psychic for them to work. You do have to have an open mind and believe they can work, however.

Dowsing Rods – "I know very well that many scientists consider dowsing as they do astrology, as a type of ancient superstition. According to my conviction this is, however, unjustified. The dowsing rod is a simple instrument which shows the reaction of the human nervous system to certain factors which are unknown to us at this time." – Albert Einstein

Dowsing Rods, Divining Rods, Witching Rods, they are all the same; they are just called different things by different areas. They were first used in Egypt over 2000 years ago to find water. They have been used to find everything from water to gold, to power lines, and yes, used to find ghosts. They are made out of many different materials, such as a tree branch, copper, steel, aluminum, or a combination of materials. The thing about dowsing rods is that they do take total concentration on what you are looking for. If you are out there hunting ghosts and you are thinking about getting something to eat, they will probably direct you to the nearest burger joint. And they don't work for everyone. If you are one of the people they do work for, you can not only look for the ghosts, but you can also communicate with them. To communicate, you just ask simple questions like, "Are you here?" If so, please move the rods to the right—something like that.

Smudging Herbs – For those of you that don't know, "smudging" is a Native American method for cleansing the body of negative energy. It is said that before you can be healed or heal someone else, you have to be purified yourself. There are many different herbs used in smudging, each with its own reasons and effects. Look them up if you're interested. A few of them are sage, sweetgrass, and cedar. These items can be bought online at a pretty cheap price.

Pendulum – A pendulum is a simple tool used for communicating and gaining guidance from the spiritual world. It is a lanyard with some sort of crystal or stone on end. The pendulum acts as an antenna that amplifies signals or energy vibrations emanating from a spiritual guide or the divine energies you've called upon. These vibrations focus their attention on the pendulum and cause it to move in specific directions, giving you answers and guidance to the questions you put to the tool.

These are just a few of the tools used in the metaphysical branch of paranormal investigations. There are more tools that can be utilized.

If the metaphysical part of the paranormal interests you, there are plenty of places you can go to dig deeper into the metaphysical world to understand it better and learn what the tools are used for and how to use them.

TYPES OF HAUNTINGS

All hauntings and activities are not the same. There are a few different types of hauntings. In this chapter, I am going to define and tell you about the different types of "Hauntings" that you may come across in your various investigations, depending on just how deep you want to get into this field.

Residual haunting - Residual hauntings are probably the most common type of haunting there is. They can't see you, hear you, or communicate with you. They are an imprint of energy from the past. It's kind of like watching a DVD on repeat. Meaning it's a scene playing over and over again through the years. Many of the locations where this type of haunting occurs experienced an event or a series of events, which imprinted itself on the atmosphere of a place. The events are not always visual either. They are often replayed as sounds or noises that have no explanation. A good example of a residual is when I was 12, my family moved into a very old house, and every night at about 9 pm, we heard a door slam. The sound came from right in front of my bedroom by the door. Trust me, when you are 12, that is not what you want to hear. We never saw anything. We ended up naming him Charlie and would say Charlie's home when the door slammed.

Often, but not always, the sounds and images recorded at certain locations are related to traumatic events that took place and caused some sort of disturbance. Trauma and emotion evoke and create higher than normal energy. That is why people report seeing and hearing things in a lot of the battlefields and cemeteries all over the place. Other times images have been created out of repetitive actions that cause an energy impression. That is why a lot of people report seeing apparitions going up and downstairs and are often mistaken as intelligent hauntings. But one big difference between this type of residual and an intelligent haunting is, there is no interaction with the living.

Intelligent haunting - An intelligent haunting is the spirit/ghost of someone who has not crossed over into heaven or into the light. They stayed here. They are called earth-bound spirits. A few of the reasons they might have stayed here are: They died in a sudden and tragic manner, such as war, and they don't know they are dead, or they may be trapped in our world. They may even feel a particularly strong bond with a specific location or person and choose to come back to be at the location or with the person. Probably the most common example of an intelligent haunting is when someone passes away, they will stick around long enough to make sure their loved ones are going to be ok. As a paranormal investigator, I've had countless people giving me accounts of a loved one who had visited them after they passed. One that comes to mind was when a lady was telling me about her mother's passing. There was a family get-together at her sister's house, and around 10:00 pm, her five-year-old nephew had got out of bed and walked up to her and asked if she could go get Grandma and bury her next to his aunt because she was bugging him, and he couldn't sleep. Grandma was in the next state over. Everyone knew grandma had been sick, but nobody knew she had died. Everyone who was especially close to Grandma had received some sort of sign from her before the funeral, then after the funeral, nothing else happened.

Non-human entities - Ok, this is where the paranormal field really starts to spread out. Non-human entities are fairly rare. There are several different types of non-human entities:

Poltergeist – Poltergeist is German for noisy ghost or spirit. A poltergeist is an entity that is responsible for physical disturbances such as loud noises, objects being moved or destroyed, and has been reported to, bite, trip, push and pinch people. Most reports of poltergeist activity include objects being moved or levitating. Most but not all poltergeist activity takes place around girls of puberty age with some sort of emotional trauma going on. There have been reports of puberty-aged boys and even older adults as well. The majority have no idea they are causing this.

Angels - Angels are spiritual beings, messengers of God. They do not usually have a human form. When they have been seen, they have been described as bright light, and the person's experiencing this described comforting feelings.

Demons – Demons are extremely rare and are malevolent spirits that cause all sorts of hate and discontent, including but not limited to bodily harm, possession, and property damage. Demonic hauntings usually start out fairly subtle. They typically have the same behavior as a poltergeist, maybe a little more extreme. It is possible for more than one demonic entity to exist in the same location. Demons are evil, supernatural beings of intelligence and are extremely powerful. They are seen as black masses standing in doorways or in the corner of the room. If you do come across a demonic situation, DO NOT try to handle yourself! You need to contact a demonologist; unless you are a trained demonologist, you could definitely cause more harm than good.

Animal spirits – This is a difficult one. There are plenty of people out there that say animals have no soul; therefore, there cannot be animal spirits/ghosts. I say, how can animals have no soul when there are so many accounts of an animal in mourning? I don't believe you can mourn if you have no soul. Then you have the Native American belief in Animal Spirit Guides. The animal guide offers their wisdom and power with whom they are communicating with conveying respect and trust. To get any deeper into the Native American belief of Animal Spirit Guides is a totally different subject.

There have been many discussions about the different types of non-human entities, and I'm sure there will be many more. Depending on where your interests are, you can dig deeper into the subject of non-human entities.

TYPES OF OCCURRENCES

There are several different types of occurrences you can expect to experience during your investigations. Not all during the same investigation, but anything is possible. There will be some investigations you will not experience anything. Here are some of the types of manifestations you will come across with the different types of hauntings

(Photo courtesy of John Stephens)

Shadow figures / people -This is probably one of the more controversial types of occurrences. You have the people who totally do not believe in shadow figures, saying that they are nothing more than manmade shadows or sleep deprivation, or drug & alcohol-induced. Then the people who do believe in shadow figures don't agree either. Some people believe they are part of the Non-human Entity category and that they are evil demons out to cause harm. Some people believe they are Intelligent Hauntings in a different form. Personally, I think they can be both, and you have to take them on a case-by-case basis.

During one investigation in Colonial Williamsburg with Cherie Bryant, we were walking down the street in front of the Governor's Palace near midnight when Cherie saw a human-shaped shadow figure in front of the palace walls. She pointed it out to me. We watched it walk off to the left. We went to see where it had gone to, but there was a wall there, and it would have been impossible for a live human to go in the direction we observed the shadow figure going.

ORBS - Some people call them ghost orbs or spirit orbs. Whatever you want to call them, approximately 98% of the orbs you catch with a camera can be explained away. It's some sort of reflection: dust, bugs, moisture, or something like that. In fact, when it comes to outdoor pictures and orbs, I discount probably 100% of the orb pictures. There are several different websites that show different examples of explainable orbs such as dust, bugs, pollen, etc. True orbs are fairly rare. A true orb puts off its own light and can usually be seen with your eyes if you just so happen to be looking in the direction of the orb. In all the investigations I've ever been on, there have only been two orbs I have ever come across that I would consider paranormal. They both just happen to come from the same location—a 280-year-old plus plantation manor house in Williamsburg, VA. One I actually saw with my own eyes. I was in the basement with three other gentlemen. An orb appeared in front of us and moved up the stairs and disappeared. Unfortunately, the DVR camera was pointed in the wrong direction, and I was unable to get that one on video. However, the second one I was able to catch on video.

(Figure 6 Video still of an orb un-abled to be debunked)

(Figure 7 The grave of Eliza Ward. She died in 1849 in Williamsburg, Virginia.)

Full body apparitions – Full/Partial body manifestations are fairly rare, but they do occur. The images are human, sometimes animal, where the subject is fully or partially formed and somewhat transparent. In some cases, the manifestation is clear enough to where friends or family can recognize the person if they are around when the manifestation occurs. If caught in a picture or video, this would be considered the Holy Grail of ghost hunting, especially if you were able to have a recorded conversation at the same time.

Phantom smells – Many people have experienced phantom smells, mysterious scents that appear seemingly out of nowhere — commonly reported smells include perfume, flowers, cigarette/cigar/pipe smoke, and fire.

Disembodied voices – For the majority of cases, the only time you will hear voices (unless you are a psychic) is when you are listening to your recordings, audio, or video. However, there are times when the energy is just right, and everything is perfect; you will be able to hear sounds, voices, or even actual words with your own ears. When this happens, I truly hope you are recording it. If you are, make sure you "tag" it on the recording, and hopefully, you are able to catch it as well.

Electronic Voice Phenomena (**EVPs**) – When you are unable to hear the disembodied voices with your own ears, you may be able to catch something with your voice recorder or by using a ghost/spirit box or some other electronic device. There are three categories of EVPs. They are as follows:

Class A – Loud, clear, and easy to understand without the use of headphones.

Class B – You are able to hear something without headphones, but normally you will have to use the headphones to understand what is being said.

Class C – Faint sounds; you can hear something with headphones but are unable to understand or make out any specific words. Sometimes you will be able to use computer software to clean up background noises, and you will just be able to make out a word or two.

Mean spirits – I'm not going to sit here and tell you that everything is always going to be fun and exciting. It's not. If you do this long enough, you will come across an angry ghost or mean spirit. For the most part, if you stay respectful and you don't try to taunt them, everything will be ok. But, as I said, you will come across one or two. A good rule of thumb is if they were a mean/evil person in life, more than likely, they could be a mean/evil spirit in death. Depending on what kind of energy they are able to muster up, you could experience anything from malevolent feelings and angry sounds and words up to and including physical contacts such as a push or scratch. This is a perfect reason why, before every investigation, you need to ground yourself, protect yourself in the light. Say your prayers. All religions have some sort of prayer to protect you from evil. If you do come across a mean spirit/ghost, don't try to provoke it and get it mad at you. Unless you are specially trained for situations like this, nothing good will come out of it. Even though they are rare, you have to be mindful that you may have come across a demon of some sort. It is best to just leave it alone and get some help from someone who is more qualified to deal with these things.

Moving objects – Every so often, you could actually witness a moving object. For that reason alone, you need to make sure you are always recording. My camcorder is my best friend on an investigation. Face it, who is going to believe you when you tell them you saw a glass sliding across a table unless you have video proof of it happening?

Physical touching – Though it is fairly rare for a person, such as me, without any type of special gift or psychic ability to feel physical contact with a ghost/spirit, it does happen.

During an investigation with two ladies from my team, Michelle Bennett and Vicki Wunderale, at an old plantation manor house in Williamsburg, Virginia, we had heard the name Murphy. We had investigated this location several times and had not heard this name before. We asked if Murphy was from there or came to the manor house. We heard the words come to. We asked a few more questions and were unable to make out what was said. Then we asked, do you need help crossing over into the light? And we heard the word "Help." I told him I would get him help, and then all of a sudden, I felt two cold touches, one on each forearm. To me, it felt like Murphy was saying thank you to me. About a week later, I was able to take a preacher up to the room where we had made contact with Murphy. The preacher said a prayer and was able to help Murphy cross over through the light. I have spoken with Murphy since, and I've investigated that location many times since then.

RESEARCH

The research can be the most time-consuming part of an investigation next to the data review. For some people, it is one of the more enjoyable parts of an investigation. Some people choose to research before the investigation, while others choose to do so after. Either way is correct. One of the positives about researching after your investigation is you are able to go into the investigation somewhat blind. Meaning you don't have anything to influence you, even subconsciously. Obviously, you will have to know a certain amount ahead of time, especially if you are investigating at a private residence. Even then, that information can be held back from everyone except the person conducting the initial interview with the client.

If your investigation is a private residence, the first part of your research will be with the client. Either on the phone or by email. I have a questionnaire I send to all potential clients when they first contact me. I explain to them some questions may get a little personal, and if they do not feel comfortable answering some of the questions, that is perfectly all right. The more questions they can answer, the better off you are as an investigator. After I receive the questionnaire back, I set up a phone interview and go over their answers and make whatever notes are pertinent. Then I will set up a time for an initial walk-through of the property, take a few pictures of the lay out and take more notes. The initial walk-through is a very important step. First, you get a feel for the location and learn the layout. Second, there have been a few 'hauntings' I was able to debunk and clear up just on the initial walk-through. That saves everyone involved several hours of time.

Now that you have finished with the preliminary questions and walk-throughs, you may need to do some further research. Depending on the claims and the location, there are quite a few places you can check the history and try to corroborate claims of activity, such as local historians, the public, library, city records, as well as eyewitness accounts. Most of your research can be done for free, and any part that may have a cost will be minimal.

David, Jason, and Jonathan searching old records on the USS North Carolina, WWII era battleship

THE INVESTIGATION

Ok, you've got the equipment you need, you have found a location and have obtained permission to be there after dark, and you have done your research. Now it's time to put on the fancy black T-shirt and go investigate.

Ghost hunting day or night? I have been asked many times if it was true that the ghost hunt was performed at night because that is when all the ghosts are out? I am here to tell you that is completely false. If a place is haunted, it is haunted during the day as well as at night. Everyone has heard about 3 am being the 'witching hour.' Well, that is just an ole wives tale. There is no evidence whatsoever to give any validity to that saying. The vast majority of the investigations take place at night for some of the following reasons. You get less chance of human contamination at night than you do during the day. At night most people are at home watching TV or something, so they won't be out walking around, talking loudly, and casting shadows that can contaminate any data collected. And have you ever noticed when you are in the dark, and you can't see that your other senses are heightened? You can hear a little better; you can also feel the changes in your surroundings. That all helps you with your investigation. Also, quite simply, it's easier on everyone's schedule to do it at night. Most people have jobs, and it would be difficult at best for everyone involved to get the same time off for an investigation.

It's always best when you are new to this to hook up with an established group or team so you can learn the ins and outs, dos, and don'ts of ghost hunting, but if there is not a group close to you and you want to start your own group. Do not automatically start doing private residences. The inexperienced investigator can definitely do more harm than good. Stick with going to public locations. There are quite a few places out there that will let your group investigate for a fee. I was part of a group that investigated the USS North Carolina in Wilmington, North Carolina. The fee was $800 dollars, and that sounds like a lot, but with everyone on the investigation, it was really affordable, and we had a great investigation, and it didn't break the bank. After you get quite a few investigations under your belt and you have studied this stuff, you can start doing private residences if you feel comfortable enough to do them. Assuming you are going to be part of a group, the group will need to get a game plan together. If you are going to be using a DVR system, you will need to figure out where you are going to want to set the cameras up. You also don't want to step all over everyone, so make sure to split up into groups of two or three and stay as far away from the other teams as possible so you don't contaminate any data collected. If it is a smaller location, it's a good idea for a couple of you to go out for a bit while a couple stays back at the command station to monitor the DVR system. You can swap out every 30 to 45 minutes. Actually, monitoring the DVR system is a really good idea in any investigation; you can have eyes on what is going in the different locations, and if you can see something, you can write down the time and location so the ones who are reviewing the video will know to keep a close eye out. You can also let the team that is out know what you're saying, and if they are not busy in another location, they can beat feet to where you saw something.

There are several different techniques being used in paranormal investigating, and it's always a good idea to use multiple techniques in the same investigation. That way, you can build a database for future references.

If it is raining or snowing and you are scheduled to do an outdoor ghost hunt, reschedule it. You cannot conduct a proper investigation in these conditions. You will not be able to take any video or conduct any EVP sessions because of in interference the rain and snow will cause. When it's foggy, you could conduct an EVP session, but any video you took would not be any good. Besides, when it's raining and snowing, you will be pretty miserable out in there.

Keep an open mind. Without an open mind, it will be a lot easier to miss something that may be happening right near you. Any negative feelings may drive the spirits away. Also, negative energy could attract a negative entity that you don't want or are not ready for. While being open-minded, you must be skeptical at the same time. Look for causes for any phenomenon, such as natural or manmade causes. As an investigator, you have to make sure your final evidence will stand up to scrutiny. By eliminating all other explanations, your evidence becomes stronger proof.

Be respectful of the locations. Unless you are investigating your own property, this is a huge rule more than a tip. There are a lot of locations that are really skeptical about letting paranormal investigators into a location for one reason or another. And if you go desecrating it somehow, you will have to pay to fix it. You will also ensure a responsible investigative team or group will not be allowed to conduct any investigations in the future. Finally, the negative energy that is produced when you are being disrespectful of a location could cause more problems than you may be prepared for.

Here are some of the techniques you can use during your investigation.

Provoking – Ok, let's get this one out of the way right off the bat. There are a couple of TV shows out there that have kind of glorified provoking as an investigative technique. Plain and simply

DON'T DO IT! The way I tell people who ask me, I'm a fairly large man. I can fight a lot of things. But you cannot fight this. They don't fight fair. They fight to win! If the only way I am able to make contact with a ghost is to make it mad at me, then I don't want to make contact with them. It can be dangerous, and it's just plain disrespectful even if you are in prison trying to make contact with a convicted killer or rapist. They are dead, and they have paid their debt, so give them the same respect you would want for yourself. On one investigation I was on, there was a young woman there, late teens or early twenties. She was performing an EVP session. She was just starting to be a bit disrespectful, making some inappropriate comments, when she asked, "Is there anything you want to tell us?" Then, over the speaker, we all heard it plain as day say "@#&! off!" She got scared and left. So, it's best to just not provoke.

Evp sessions – An EVP session is the cornerstone of all paranormal investigations/ghost hunts. An EVP session is combined with all other techniques of investigation, whether you are just using a voice recorder or a video camera. If you do not have a voice recorder or video camera documenting what is happening, then it is just a personal experience, and like I said before. Personal experiences are exciting, but they are not evidence.

The number one rule in conducting an EVP session is speaking in a normal voice. Do not whisper. It takes long enough to go through all the audio files. When you whisper, you make it difficult on whoever is reviewing the audio files from your investigation. They may have a hard time trying to determine if it's a ghost or human, and when they do figure it out, they will not be too happy to find out they had just wasted time trying to figure out what you said vs. going on to other audio files that may actually have paranormal contact.

When conducting an EVP session, you want to start off by 'Marking' the date, time, and location of the session, i.e., "David and

Emily, EVP session September 5, 2021, at the John Doe residence, in the master bedroom." Then, depending on what the history and claims are, you just start asking all sorts of questions in a regular conversational voice. "Hello, my name is David. What is your name?" something like that. When you are doing an EVP session, you need to make sure you are not shooting off rapid-fire questions. You need to give the ghosts time to respond. A good rule of thumb is to wait 15-30 seconds between questions.

You need to remember when you hear a sound to 'Tag' it on the voice recorder, whether it's an unexplained or explained sound. "That rumbling sound was just my stomach." Or "I just heard a voice, and I don't know where it came from." That way, whoever is going over the audio files knows to ignore the sound or listen even closer to see if the voice was picked up and what was said. If you are using a video camera, either DVR or handheld, this would be a great time to add other pieces of equipment. That way, you can have video documentation if anything happens. For example, you could ask whoever it is you are communicating with to touch the REM POD. If the lights and sounds go off, you have it on video. When I'm doing an EVP session, I do part of it with a ghost box and part of it without. There have been times when I have not got anything with a ghost box but was able to get something without the ghost box and vice versa.

When you are at a public location, where they have had many ghost hunts previously, whatever ghosts or spirits that may be there might not want to answer the same old questions everyone always asks. You may want to change up the questions. Meaning, you can ask the normal everyday questions everyone else asks. What's your name, how old are you, how did you die, etc. Ask different questions that are not normally asked. Such as, 'do you have any children?' 'What's your wife's/husband's name?' 'What type of activities do you enjoy?' etc.

Some friends of mine and fellow paranormal investigators recently had a conversation about a location here in Virginia near Richmond. The Cabin on 360, where during one investigation, just about the only activity they were able to get that night was adult in nature. Now the Cabin on 360 has had many other occurrences over the year; it was just this night the ghosts didn't feel like answering any of the other questions.

So, do not be afraid of changing up the subject matter. If the ghosts/spirits you are looking for are from a certain time period, by all means, talk about that time period. But also talk about different time periods as well. There may be a ghost/spirit there that you weren't expecting, or maybe the ones you were expecting may be interested in talking about that as well. You never know until you try.

Confederate Kepi

Trigger objects - The use of trigger objects is just like it sounds. You are using an object, such as a toy, personal belonging, or something else associated with the deceased, in conjunction with your equipment to elicit some sort of reaction or response from the ghosts. When you are using trigger objects, you need to make sure the object pertains to whoever it is you are trying to make contact with. For example, let say you are trying to communicate with a child from the 1800s; you will want to use a child's toy, but make sure it's one they would have played with back then, like a teddy bear or something. If you set up an Xbox 360, it probably would not work too well. There are several pieces of equipment you can use in conjunction with your trigger objects. You definitely want to use your voice recorder and video camera if you have one. You can also use your EMF meter. Just set the meter on or right next to the object and see if it registers any higher EMFs. There are a few companies out there that make different pieces of equipment that you can use with or as trigger objects.

There have been instances when an investigator places a ball in a certain location, walks away, and comes back a while later that ball is somehow in a different location without explanation. As exciting as this would be, this cannot be considered evidence. After you set the ball up, you have to verify there is no way for the wind or a/c to move the ball. I actually have a REM-POD that I am able to take the antenna out and plug a cable with an alligator clip into it. I then clip the alligator clip to a metal pizza pan, and that becomes the antenna. I will place my trigger object onto the pizza pan. I have used this method several times with success. You need to also have a video camera set up because with all the other things you have in place; it's still just a really neat personal experience without documentation.

Really effective use of trigger objects is when you are able to use people and/or events. Maybe get someone in a period costume. Let's say you are in an area that is rich with Civil War history. Look up to see if there are any re-enactments happening and see if you can get permission to conduct an investigation after the day's activities are concluded. The area should be ripe with the right energy for an investigation; if you are able to be there during the re-enactment need to take as many pictures as possible with the hopes of catching a glimpse of something.

Phil Payette of Tidewater Paranormal Investigations, using himself as a trigger object in Sick Bay on the USS North Carolina.

Photography – It doesn't matter if you are still taking photos or a video. Photography can produce the most amazing evidence or cause a lot of pareidolia. Here are a few things to do and not do to help get some irrefutable evidence.

No smoking at the location; this can appear like a mist in the photos. You don't want to contaminate your evidence.

Watch for air-born contaminates being stirred up in the area you are photographing. They will produce 'Orbs,' and that can negate any true orbs that you may catch. When you set up, you will want to wait several minutes before you start taking photos or videos to give any dust, dander, or anything else to settle down. Keep an eye out for any cobwebs that may be moving with the breeze.

All long hair should be tied back or under a hat.

Don't bother with your camera's viewfinder. Hold the camera out in front of you and aim at the area you want to take a picture of. This helps in cold weather by keeping your camera away from your breath.

Watch for reflective surfaces and make notes of them. The flash reflected off shiny surfaces such as windows, polished tombstones, etc., can look light an orb or other anomaly. Make a note of streetlights and any other light source that may appear in the picture. Sometimes you will see an orb, mist, or sparkles in your flash or other flashes, take more pictures right there; you may be near a ghost.

In cold weather, be conscious of your breath, so you don't photograph that; it'll look like mist or vapor.

Do your best to eliminate any false positive pictures. That way, the skeptics and non-believers will have little to no ammunition to discredit your findings.

Let fellow investigators know when you are taking a photo. If you are using flash photography in the dark and the people you are with who are looking in your direction when you take the picture, you won't be too happy by looking directly into the flash. And also, be careful that you don't get double flashes. If you think you have a double flash photo or any other false positive, log the picture number so you can exclude that photo from the batch when you are reviewing the collected data.

Some people like to ask the ghosts if they can take their pictures before they start shooting. It can't hurt.

Take pictures anywhere and everywhere. It's a good idea to take multiple pictures of the same location, one right after the other. That way, you can compare them. You can never take too many pictures. It's better to take hundreds of photos and delete 95% of them because there was nothing there than to just take a few photos and risk missing an amazing piece of evidence. If you feel something or someone else does. Take a picture. Did you think you saw something? Take a picture. Take photos whenever you get a positive reading on any piece of equipment. With technology these days, it's a really good idea to use a good camcorder or body cam. A lot of the video editing software out there lets you take stills from a video. A DVR system is great for this as well as long as you remember to have it set up for the best quality video. Preferably 1080p or higher that way, you can get the clearest picture possible. Anything lower than 1080P starts getting grainy. You can review the DVR footage right on the DVR with a good monitor and take stills from there.

USING EMF METERS – The theory behind EMF meters in the paranormal is the ghosts put off a slight electromagnetic field, hence the use of an EMF meter. As I showed earlier, there are quite a few different types of EMF meters. They are all pretty much the same, but however, they do have different bells and whistles to make them a little different. When you are using an EMF meter, you must be extremely careful of your surroundings. You have to be mindful of any object that will have the ability to give off a false positive reading on your meter, such as a breaker box, outlets, light switches, lamps, TVs, stereos, your cell phone, faulty wiring, etc. That is why you must make sure to do a baseline reading before you start in each location.

Depending on the type of meter you are using at the time, you can use the EMF meter as the focal point of a part of your investigation or in conjunction with another piece of equipment. If you are using a meter as a focal point, it would be a good idea to use one that lights up and can be seen from a distance, such as a REM-POD or one of the many other types that light up and make sounds

During one investigation a few years ago on board an old WWII battleship, the USS North Carolina, in Wilmington, North Carolina. I was with two other gentlemen, Jason Britt and Jonathan Elliot Foley. We were walking through the Chief's passageway (E7 and above), talking about how we both were E5's. All of a sudden, our EMF meters started to spike. We started asking questions and were getting direct responses to our questions. Apparently, whoever was there didn't care for some E5 just casually strolling through their passageway.

The use of psychics on an investigation – First off, I want to get one thing right out in the open. I do believe there are some people who have the gift of being able to feel, see, hear, or communicate with the spirit world. I am not one of them by any stretch of the imagination. However, I am also one of the biggest skeptics out there. If I had a dollar for every person who has come up to me saying; I'm a sensitive, an empath, a psychic, or whatever, I'd be a rich man. I know two people personally that have a gift of some sort of psychic abilities that I trust on an investigation and would definitely listen to what they have to say. The rest I just take with a grain of salt until they can prove to me that they are what they say they are. I don't call them out because I may very well be wrong in my assessment of them. I just won't ask them for their opinions on an investigation. I do believe that if a person is in the paranormal field long enough, they could develop a certain sensitivity but that by no means makes them sensitive or an empath.

The term psychic is a fairly loose term. There are several types of psychics out there. You have empaths who feel emotion. Sensitives who can just feel the presence of something there. Mediums who are able to hear and feel thoughts or voices from the spirit world. Then you have clairvoyants who are able to actually interact with the spirit world. These are the ones you come across mostly. There are others. Some have the ability to auto-write, meaning the spirit almost takes over and controls the writer's hand.

The psychics I have come across, either on TV or in person, will go into an investigation completely blind. That way, if they do come up with something that can corroborate a claim, you can't say they only said that because they knew of it beforehand. So, if you are fortunate enough to be able to investigate with someone who actually does have abilities, make sure you have at the very least a voice recorder on them but preferably a video camera.

If you are on a private residence investigation and you decide to use a psychic, make completely sure you trust this person as a psychic. If they are not what they say, they could definitely cause more harm than good, depending on what they claim their abilities are and what they try to accomplish.

53

54

55

56

REVIEW AND REVEAL

Reviewing the Data: Ok, now that you have got the fieldwork done, you have rested up from being out all night; it's time to get to review all the data you collected. Hopefully, you will have help with this part of the investigation. The review will take longer than any other part of the investigation. You need to look at all the notes you or any of the other investigators took, video, and still pictures, as well as listen to all the audios. This part of the investigation can be very tedious and sometimes downright boring. But it is probably one of the most important parts of the investigation. It is important because assuming you are going to post your findings somewhere or if you are conducting an investigation for a private residence, you need to make sure that you are presenting actual evidence and not something false that can be torn apart.

There are several computer software programs out there to help with going through the audio. You can isolate certain sounds and noises to try and determine if it's paranormal or if there is some sort of natural explanation. Same with video files. When you get to a certain part of the video that you think you saw something or you have a note where one of the other investigators saw or heard something, you can slow the video down and go through it frame by frame to check out what may have been captured on the video.

When going through the still pictures, you should enlarge the pictures to help to determine if the possible anomaly is what it actually seems to be or if there is some sort of natural explanation. But you need to be sure not to enlarge too much because you can then cause distortion, and you could either dismiss an actual anomaly or think you have something that you don't.

Revealing the Evidence: Once you've gone through everything and you've gotten second and third opinions on potential evidence. Now is the time to reveal the findings if you so choose. We all know there are many places to post your findings, from Facebook to YouTube to online forums to your own website. Fair warning, if you do choose to post your findings on the net, you will need to have thick skin and be prepared to have whatever evidence you post to be torn apart. Most people will be pretty respectful and point out flaws in your findings which invites constructive discussion about the evidence and future investigative techniques. Then you will have the people out there who are jerks and live to make other people feel bad, that even without taking a good look at the evidence, will call it fake. There are some people who are so closed-minded that you could be posting a picture of you shaking hands with a full-body apparition, and you have witnesses that saw it happen; they would still say it was a fake, or you have no clue of what you are talking about. You need to ignore those people. A lot of them are just jealous that they have never caught anything that could not be debunked.

AUTHOR'S NOTE

I just want to say thank you for taking the time to read the previous pages. I sincerely hope I was able to give you a little insight into the field of the paranormal and that you were able to learn and take something away from the time you spent reading this. Below is my contact information in case you have any questions or comments.

Thank you again, and happy ghost hunting.

David A. Flowers
Founder and lead investigator
Virginia Paranormal Occurrence Research
Vapor757.David@aol.com
Facebook.com/vapor757

PARANORMAL GLOSSARY / DICTIONARY

Anomaly: Something that deviates from the norm or from expectations, something strange and difficult to identify or classify.

Attachment: The seeming connection a haunting or entity may have with an item, such as furniture or other personal belonging. Often, this type of haunting is noticed when an item is first brought into a location. When the item is again removed, the events related to the haunting will cease.

Apparition: An appearance of a supposed ghost; something or somebody strange and/or unexpected.

Cold Spots: Are referred to in connection with paranormal activity are not the drafty currents you feel in old houses or even new houses, for that matter. They are a sudden drop in temperature and only take up a specific area.

Debunk: To show something wrong or false when an investigator finds a simple and logical explanation for paranormal activity. Just because certain things can be debunked doesn't mean there is no paranormal activity; it just means that those portions of the activity may be ruled out as paranormal.

Disembodied Voice: A voice heard during an investigation, but a source could not be found.

Electromagnetic Field: Also known as an EMF.

Electromagnetic Radiation is energy that, as it penetrates the surrounding areas, creates EMFs. All electronics, appliances, power wires, and power lines produce EMFs. At higher levels, EMFs can cause health issues and ill effects to humans. A spike of an EMF from an unknown is theorized to be a ghost/spirit.

Entity: A generic term used to define paranormal spirit.

E.V.P: Electronic Voice Phenomena, disembodied 'voices' and sounds imprinted on audio recording devices that are not heard by the human ear. EVP's are the most common type of evidence a paranormal investigator collects.

Exorcism: Ceremonial expulsion of invading spiritual/demonic entities from a person or dwelling, present in virtually every worldly culture. The Jewish and Catholic Christian faiths each have a formal 'Rite of Exorcism' to be conducted by the respective Rabbi or Priest.

False Positive: When a photo, video, or some kind of meter spike can be discredited as being something natural or manmade.

Ghost: The image of a person witnessed after his/her death, reflecting the appearance of the living, physical body yet less substantial. These forms often seem to exist in a dream-like state of semi-awareness, at times though not always cognizant of their human observers.

Hitchhiker: This is when a ghost, spirit, or entity (former human and/or non-human variety) follows an investigator home from a location.

Haunting: The manifestation of a ghostly presence, or presence, attached to a specific locale. A haunting can be categorized into many distinct types.

Hot Spot: An area or location of higher or frequent activity of paranormal activity.

Light Anomaly: A true paranormal 'orb' that is viewed with the naked eye. There is believed to be energy that is tied to a ghost/spirit. The true source of energy is unknown.

Materialization: A ghost appearing visually, suddenly or gradually, sometimes indistinct, sometimes seemingly quite solid. (See also apparition)

Matrixing: When the mind starts seeing familiar patterns in things. Like when you look at a cloud and see familiar shapes like faces and animals, that's matrixing. The human mind has a natural tendency to interpret sensory input (also known as pareidolia).

Occult: Relating to the paranormal, the definition in simple terms would mean the supernatural, magic, witchcraft, or devil worship.

Ouija Board: Pronounced "wee-gee" a trademark "game" board with letters, numbers, and other symbols and a pointer called a planchette with answers to questions are spelled out by supposedly spiritual forces. DO NOT BE FOOLED; THIS IS NOT A GAME. This is thought to be a portal to another realm where the entities have been known to be negative. Experienced researchers vehemently advise against their usage.

Orb: In theory, orbs are a form of energy of unknown sources which are believed to be disembodied spirits. True spirit orbs emit their own energy source or light and are rare. Most orbs found in paranormal investigations are just dust or bugs caught in the light of the cameras. Basically, if it can be recreated by shaking a towel or flannel shirt, it can't be taken seriously.

Paranormal: An event that is unable to be explained or understood in terms of scientific knowledge.

Pareidolia: A psychological phenomenon involving a stimulus (an image or a sound) wherein the mind perceives a familiar pattern of something where none actually exists (Also called Matrixing)

Pentacle / Pentagram: The traditional five-pointed star design, with its interior pentagon delineated.

Possession: Invasion of the human mind by a spiritual or demonic entity, where the invading agent for a span of time influences or entirely subverts the personality of the human host. It is in these instances that the boundaries of psychology, religion, and spiritualism are rendered less distinct.

Preternatural: It is that which appears beyond or outside of the normal. In contrast to the supernatural, preternatural phenomenon are presumed to have natural explanations that are yet unknown.

Spirit: The essence, energy, or soul of a living or deceased person, animal, or being. A spirit commonly refers to a ghost.

Spirit Rescue: Attempting contact with entities, intended to alleviate the entities' distress and aid them in the resolution of their conflicts and in 'crossing over' to a higher, spiritual plane.

Supernatural: Is that which is above or beyond that which one holds to be natural or exists outside natural law and the observable universe.